Owen's Day with Daddy written by Jerry Ruff and illustrated by Davilyn Lynch

ISBN 978-1-60537-644-8

This book was printed in April 2022 at Nikara,
M. R. Štefánika 858/25, 963 01 Krupina, Slovakia.

First Edition
10 9 8 7 6 5 4 3 2 1

Clavis Publishing supports the First Amendment and celebrates the right to read.

Owen's Day with Daddy

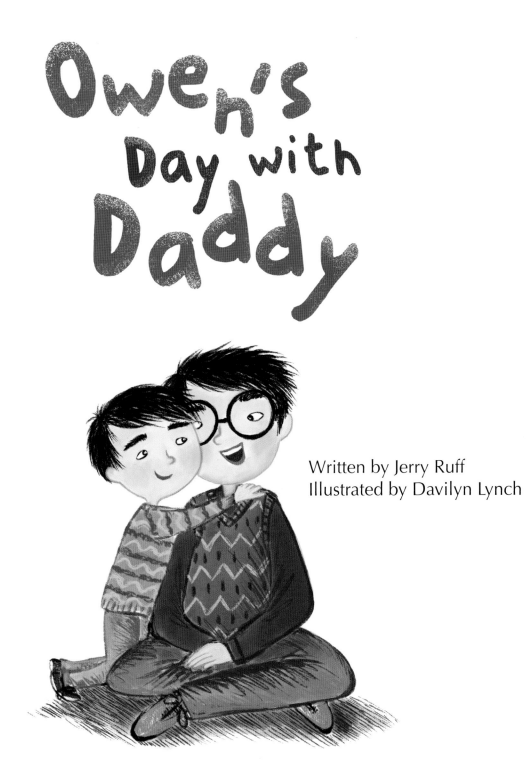

Written by Jerry Ruff
Illustrated by Davilyn Lynch

Clavis

NEW YORK

Owen's daddy was holding the baby.

He made sounds for the baby
with his tongue.

"Cluck, cluck."

He smiled at the baby.
He said, "How ya' doing, little man?"

He kissed the baby
right on the head.

Owen stomped his foot and yelled,

"I want to do something with you, Daddy!"

The baby started to cry.

"My tummy feels sick," Owen said when everything was calm again.

"I'm sorry to hear that," said Daddy.

"Do you still want to do something?"

"Like what?" said Owen.
Then he had an idea.
"Not one thing.
Three things."

"Okay," said Daddy. "Three things. What's the first thing?"
Owen thought about it. "The park."

At the park, the ducks swam in the pond.
"Duck, duck, hungry duck!" Daddy called.
"Duck, duck, hungry duck!" Owen called.

"Duck, duck

hungry duck!"

Daddy took the bag of dried corn from his pocket.

He poured some corn into Owen's hand.

"Lunch time, munch time!" Daddy called.
He tossed some corn on the grass.

"Lunch time, munch time!" Owen called,
and he tossed some corn on the grass, too.

A momma duck and six baby ducks waddled over.
They gobbled up the corn.

"You feed the babies," Daddy said.
He poured more corn into Owen's hand.
"I'll feed the momma."

Owen sprinkled corn by his feet.
The babies came right up and ate it.

He put a piece of corn on the toe of his shoe.
One of the babies snatched it.

He put a piece of corn in the middle of his hand
and held it out. A baby duck ate it!

"It ate the corn on my hand!"
Owen shouted. "It likes you!" said Daddy.

When the corn was gone,
Daddy crunched up the bag.
"What's next?" he asked Owen.
Owen thought about it.
"The playground."

The playground had two slides, a big slide and a little slide.

"Which slide today?" Daddy asked.

Owen thought about it.

The ladder on the big slide went up and up.

One time, Owen had started climbing, but it was too high.

He began to cry and his daddy carried him down.

"That one," said Owen,
pointing to the little slide.
Then he thought some more.
"No, that one," he said,
pointing to the big slide this time.

Owen stood by the ladder. He looked up.

His head felt funny. His tummy felt funny.

He touched the ladder. It was cold.

"I'll be right behind you," Daddy said.

Together, Owen and his daddy climbed the ladder.
At the top, Daddy said, "You can sit on my lap."
When they were ready, Daddy said,
"Let's count. One—two—three!"

"1, 2, 3!"

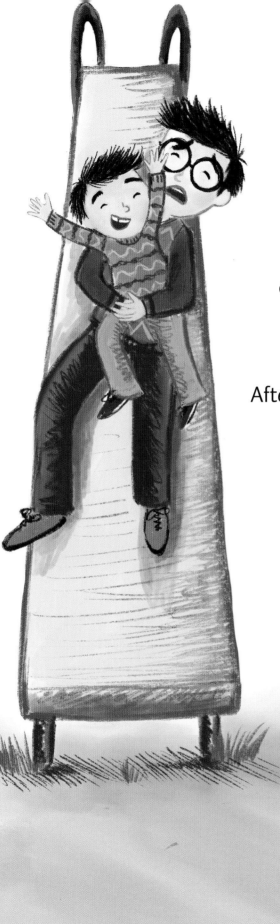

Down they went!
Owen screamed! His daddy screamed!
When their feet touched the ground,
Owen shouted, "Again!"

"Weeeeeeeeeeeee!"

After three more times, Daddy said,
"It's almost lunch time.
What's next, Owen?"
Owen thought about it.
"Cheeseburgers."

At the drive thru, Daddy asked,
"You want to give the order, Owen?"

"Three cheeseburgers, and three French fries," Owen said out the car window.
"Don't forget milkshakes," Daddy whispered.
"And three milkshakes."

On the drive home, Owen asked, "Can babies drink milkshakes?"

"No, they aren't big enough yet," Daddy said.

"I am," said Owen.

At home, Momma sat in the rocking chair.
She was feeding the baby.
"I gave the baby ducks corn," Owen said,
"and I went down the big slide."

"Wow," said Momma.
"You're growing up, Owen."

"I ordered cheeseburgers too," Owen said,
holding up the bag. "And milkshakes.
But the baby is too little
for milkshakes," he added.

Owen put the plates on the table.
Three plates.

"I think it's time for the baby's nap," Momma said.

"Can I kiss him first?" Owen asked.

"Of course," said Momma.

Owen kissed the baby, so softly,

on top of his head. Three kisses.

The baby didn't wake up.

And Owen felt very grown up, indeed.